FOR THE CHILDREN OF SAWREY

FROM

OLD MR. BUNNY

THE TALE OF
BENJAMIN BUNNY

BY

BEATRIX POTTER

AUTHOR OF "THE TALE OF PETER RABBIT," &C.

This edition is distributed by
AVENEL BOOKS
a division of Crown Publishers, Inc.

K

ONE morning a little rabbit sat on a bank.

He pricked his ears and listened to the trit-trot, trit-trot of a pony.

A gig was coming along the road; it was driven by Mr. McGregor, and beside him sat Mrs. McGregor in her best bonnet.

As soon as they had passed, little Benjamin Bunny slid down into the road, and set off—with a hop, skip, and a jump—to call upon his relations, who lived in the wood at the back of Mr. McGregor's garden.

THAT wood was full of rabbit holes; and in the neatest, sandiest hole of all lived Benjamin's aunt and his cousins—Flopsy, Mopsy, Cotton-tail, and Peter.

Old Mrs. Rabbit was a widow; she earned her living by knitting rabbit-wool mittens and muffatees (I once bought a pair at a bazaar). She also sold herbs, and rosemary tea, and rabbit-tobacco (which is what we call lavender).

LITTLE Benjamin did not very much want to see his Aunt.

He came round the back of the fir-tree, and nearly tumbled upon the top of his Cousin Peter.

PETER was sitting by him-
self. He looked poorly,
and was dressed in a red cotton
pocket-handkerchief.

"Peter," said little Benjamin, in a whisper, "who has
got your clothes?"

PETER replied, "The scarecrow in Mr. McGregor's
garden," and described how he
had been chased about the
garden, and had dropped his
shoes and coat.

Little Benjamin sat down
beside his cousin and assured
him that Mr. McGregor had
gone out in a gig, and Mrs.
McGregor also; and certainly
for the day, because she was
wearing her best bonnet.

PETER said he hoped that
it would rain.

At this point old Mrs.
Rabbit's voice was heard inside the rabbit hole, calling:
"Cotton-tail! Cotton-tail! fetch
some more camomile!"

Peter said he thought he
might feel better if he went
for a walk.

THEY went away hand in
hand, and got upon the
flat top of the wall at the bot-
tom of the wood. From here
they looked down into Mr.
McGregor's garden. Peter's
coat and shoes were plainly to
be seen upon the scarecrow,
topped with an old tam-o'-
shanter of Mr. McGregor's.

LITTLE Benjamin said: "It spoils people's clothes to squeeze under a gate; the proper way to get in is to climb down a pear-tree."

Peter fell down head first; but it was of no consequence, as the bed below was newly raked and quite soft.

IT had been sown with lettuces.

They left a great many odd little footmarks all over the bed, especially little Benjamin, who was wearing clogs.

LITTLE Benjamin said that the first thing to be done was to get back Peter's clothes, in order that they might be able to use the pocket-handkerchief.

They took them off the scarecrow. There had been rain during the night; there was water in the shoes, and the coat was somewhat shrunk.

Benjamin tried on the tam-o'-shanter, but it was too big for him.

THEN he suggested that
they should fill the pocket-
handkerchief with onions, as
a little present for his Aunt.

Peter did not seem to be
enjoying himself; he kept
hearing noises.

BENJAMIN, on the contrary, was perfectly at home, and ate a lettuce leaf. He said that he was in the habit of coming to the garden with his father to get lettuces for their Sunday dinner.

(The name of little Benjamin's papa was old Mr. Benjamin Bunny.)

The lettuces certainly were very fine.

PETER did not eat any-
thing; he said he should
like to go home. Presently he
dropped half the onions.

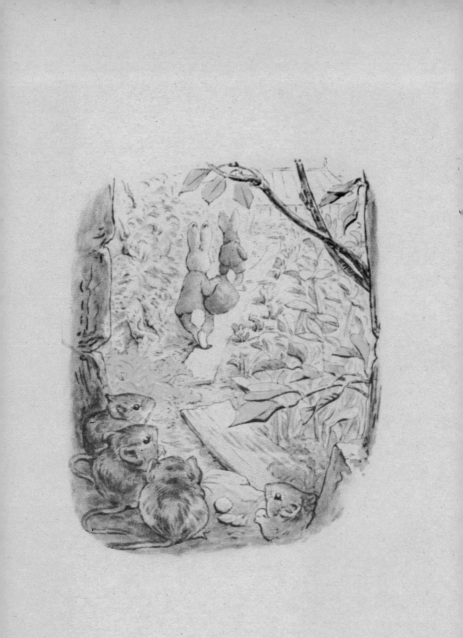

LITTLE Benjamin said that it was not possible to get back up the pear-tree with a load of vegetables. He led the way boldly towards the other end of the garden. They went along a little walk on planks, under a sunny, red brick wall.

The mice sat on their door-steps cracking cherry-stones; they winked at Peter Rabbit and little Benjamin Bunny.

PRESENTLY Peter let the
pocket-handkerchief go
again.

THEY got amongst flower-pots, and frames, and tubs. Peter heard noises worse than ever; his eyes were as big as lolly-pops!

He was a step or two in front of his cousin when he suddenly stopped.

THIS is what those little rabbits saw round that corner!

Little Benjamin took one look, and then, in half a minute less than no time, he hid himself and Peter and the onions underneath a large basket. . . .

THE cat got up and stretched herself, and came and sniffed at the basket.

Perhaps she liked the smell of onions!

Anyway, she sat down upon the top of the basket.

SHE sat there for *five hours.*

*   *   *   *   *   *

I cannot draw you a picture of Peter and Benjamin underneath the basket, because it was quite dark, and because the smell of onions was fearful; it made Peter Rabbit and little Benjamin cry.

The sun got round behind the wood, and it was quite late in the afternoon; but still the cat sat upon the basket.

AT length there was a pitter-patter, pitter-patter, and some bits of mortar fell from the wall above.

The cat looked up and saw old Mr. Benjamin Bunny prancing along the top of the wall of the upper terrace.

He was smoking a pipe of rabbit-tobacco, and had a little switch in his hand.

He was looking for his son.

OLD Mr. Bunny had no opinion whatever of cats. He took a tremendous jump off the top of the wall on to the top of the cat, and cuffed it off the basket, and kicked it into the greenhouse, scratching off a handful of fur.

The cat was too much surprised to scratch back.

WHEN old Mr. Bunny had driven the cat into the greenhouse, he locked the door.

Then he came back to the basket and took out his son Benjamin by the ears, and whipped him with the little switch.

Then he took out his nephew Peter.

T HEN he took out the
handkerchief of onions,
and marched out of the garden.

WHEN Mr. McGregor returned about half an hour later he observed several things which perplexed him.

It looked as though some person had been walking all over the garden in a pair of clogs — only the footmarks were too ridiculously little!

Also he could not understand how the cat could have managed to shut herself up *inside* the greenhouse, locking the door upon the *outside*.

WHEN Peter got home his mother forgave him, because she was so glad to see that he had found his shoes and coat. Cotton-tail and Peter folded up the pocket-handkerchief, and old Mrs. Rabbit strung up the onions and hung them from the kitchen ceiling, with the bunches of herbs and the rabbit-tobacco.

THE END